Sports for Supergirls

Cycle Sports

Louise Spilsbury

Gareth Stevens Publishing

Please visit our website, **www.garethstevens.com**.
For a free color catalog of all our high-quality books,
call toll free 1-800-542-2595 or fax 1-877-542-2596.

Cataloging-in-Publication Data

Names: Spilsbury, Louise.
Title: Cycle sports / Louise Spilsbury.
Description: New York : Gareth Stevens Publishing, 2020. | Series: Sports for supergirls | Includes glossary and index.
Identifiers: ISBN 9781538242223 (pbk.) | ISBN 9781538241950 (library bound)
Subjects: LCSH: Cycling--Juvenile literature. | Bicycle racing--Juvenile literature. | Women athletes--Juvenile literature.
Classification: LCC GV1043.5 S65 2020 | DDC 796.6--dc23

First Edition

Published in 2020 by
Gareth Stevens Publishing
111 East 14th Street, Suite 349
New York, NY 10003

Produced by Calcium
Editors: Sarah Eason and Jennifer Sanderson
Designers: Clare Webber and Jessica Moon

Photo credits: Cover: Shutterstock: Daxiao Productions; Inside: Gemma Corbera: pp. 32, 33t, 33b; Steve Diamond: pp. 1, 37t, 37b; Flickr: Puri Feijoo/fotographer of the XL-BMX (INICI -) club in Barcelone: pp. 4, 34, 35t, 42; Danny ZELCK: p. 27; Pablo Benticuaga Garcia: pp. 40, 41; Rugile Kaladyte/laelwilcox.com: pp. 14, 15t, 15b; Shutterstock: Baranq: pp. 22, 23; Bezikus: p. 5; Cristapper: p. 19t; Alex Egorov: p. 39t; ESB Professional: p. 7t; Dana Gardner: p. 11t; Des Green: p. 11b; Mitch Gunn: p. 45; Iam_Anupong: p. 24; Jacob Lund: pp. 12, 13t; Sue McDonald: p. 38; Michelangeloop : p. 39b; Pavel L Photo and Video: p. 18; Maxim Petrichuk: p. 25t; Rocketclips, Inc.: p. 7b; Rocksweeper: p. 10; Rena Schild: pp. 6, 8; Sherry V Smith: p. 35b; Chatchai Somwat: pp. 28, 29; Sportpoint: p. 25b; Tonkid: p. 13b; Gaie Uchel: pp. 17, 19b, 20; Sorapop Udomsri: pp. 3, 43; Michael Woodruff: p. 31; Wikimedia Commons: Jonas de Carvalho from Rio de Janeiro, Brasil: p. 36; Roberto Castro/brasil2016.gov.br : p. 16; Steve Fair : p. 26; Granada: p. 9b; Nicola: pp. 21t, 21b; S.Yuki: p. 9t.

CPSIA compliance information: Batch #CS19GS:
For further information contact Gareth Stevens, New York, New York at 1-800-542-2595.

Contents

Chapter 1

Girls on Wheels

Some of the more daring and extreme cycle sports are often seen as activities that are only for men. Yet today, more and more committed and fearless female riders are showing all the girls out there that this kind of riding is not just for boys.

Extreme cycle sports provide just the sort of adrenaline rush so many girls are looking for.

EXTREME CYCLE SPORTS

Girls and women have been riding bicycles to get around and for fun almost since bikes were invented. And today, they are enjoying extreme cycle sports, too. Extreme cycle sports are nothing like a gentle ride in the countryside or even a speedy ride to school. Extreme cycle sports include adventure and action, and are often daring and dangerous. They include long-distance riding, intense speed cycling, doing jumps and stunts, or speeding down rough, rocky mountainsides at breakneck speed.

A SPORT FOR ALL

The great thing about cycle sports is that anyone can do them, almost anywhere. True, there are long-distance cycle races that take place across the Arctic snow, but riders do not have to go that far to join in the fun! People can train on indoor cycle tracks or even on a stationary bike at home. They can practice tricks and stunts in city skate parks or empty garages. They can also cycle on dirt tracks in nearby countryside.

FITNESS AND FUN

Extreme cycle sports may seem like macho sports because some of them require a lot of strength, but many cycle sports require more than brute strength. They need skill and technical ability, and women can be just as good at them as men. They are also great sports for keeping fit because when riders push against the pedals to battle the air resistance trying to slow them down, they build up muscle strength.

GIRL TALK

Whatever kind of cycling people enjoy, there is one thing these sports have in common. All riders should wear a helmet. It is easy to find helmets that are light, comfortable, affordable, and stylish—so no excuses.

Getting the right helmet and other cycling gear helps riders perform well and keeps them safe and ready to enjoy another race.

On the Road

For cyclists who enjoy riding around town or getting out onto the open road on weekends, road racing can be an exciting way to take their sport to the next level. It gives riders a great thrill to feel the speed and power beneath their feet on a road and conquer rolling hills; long, slow climbs; and winding, steep descents.

TAKE TO THE ROAD

The great thing about road races is that there is a race for everyone, regardless of their age or ability. Road races vary greatly in length and location. The most popular typically take place over a single day and begin with a staggered mass start where everyone in a specific category starts together. These races are created based on distance instead of time, and range from 30 to 60 miles (48 to 97 km) long.

Most road races happen during spring and summer months, but some take place in fall and winter, too.

PACE YOURSELF

Road racers compete against other individual riders or in teams. They may start together or at staggered times. However they start, road racers will end up riding in a group. When riding in a group, it is important that riders keep a steady line so they do not crash into each other. Riders move through a pack during a race carefully, to avoid annoying or hurting other riders as they make their way to the front.

CHECK IT OUT

One of the top tips for any road racer is to make sure all their equipment is ready for the race. The last thing anyone wants is to crash out of a race because they have a mechanical fault that could have been spotted and fixed beforehand. A flat tire or faulty brakes could cost a rider their race, even if they have trained hard and are physically ready.

The key to winning a road race is preparation—and that means a lot of training!

Riders should check their equipment, from head to toe and helmet to shoes, to be confident none of it is cracked or unfit to use.

GIRL TALK

Every cyclist should keep their bicycle in tip-top condition, but even so, it is still a good idea for them to have a trusted bike mechanic check over their bike at least a week before a race.

Going the Distance

Female cyclists often struggle to have their voices heard and their talents recognized. One way riders get funding to pay for bikes and other equipment, as well as travel expenses, is through sponsorship. Sponsorship is when a company pays riders to wear or use their apparel in return for publicity. Unfortunately, female cyclists and teams get less sponsorship and support than their male counterparts. Luckily, this is changing as more female cyclists are being noticed and appreciated.

GIRL TALK

In the United States, competitive road cycling for women involves four levels, or categories, starting at Category 4 and moving up to Category 1. Competitors must earn points at specific races within a 12-month period in order to move up to the next category.

Competitive road cycling is fast and furious, and there is a lot of fierce jostling for position between riders.

Case Study

CORYN RIVERA—ELITE CYCLIST

Coryn Rivera is a Filipina-American racing cyclist who has won more than 70 national titles across road, track, cyclo-cross, and mountain biking disciplines. She is also the first-ever American, male or female, to win the Tour de Flanders, an important annual cycling race also known as the De Ronde (meaning "The Tour").

Coryn Rivera is determined to continue to develop as a professional cyclist and push herself to the limit.

EARLY START

Coryn started cycling at nine years old and very quickly realized it was the sport for her. She always felt completely comfortable and at home on a bike and loved the feeling of speed. Being a competitive person, she also loved the fact that she was so good at the sport she could usually win the races she entered. At the age of 16, she turned professional.

When she started racing full-time in 2017, Coryn won numerous races and incredibly finished sixth in the Union Cycliste Internationale (UCI) World Ranking in 2017. She thrived on the atmosphere and the huge crowds that big racing events attract. She also loves being part of a team because riders push each other to win and push themselves to the limit, no matter who the team leader is on the day of a race.

Coryn's advice to young racing cyclists is simple: Have fun, work hard, and make the most of every opportunity.

Coryn loves cycling because it is a way to explore new places and to meet friends.

Chapter 2
Endurance Racing

Cycling can be a grueling sport and never more so than in endurance cycle races. Endurance events involve long-distance races over hundreds or even thousands of miles.

Long-distance endurance cycle races test riders to the max!

ENDURANCE FORMATS

There are several different formats of endurance racing. Single-day races can go from one place to another or involve several circuits of a track. The first rider to finish wins, but racers may have handicaps so that better riders start after the others. Stage races involve several segments completed in order. The cyclist with the shortest cumulative time across all the stages wins, although there may be winners for particular stages, or categories of stages (such as the mountain stage).

EXTREME ENDURANCE

Some endurance races are more extreme than others. There can be 24-hour races against the clock, called time trials, or even highest annual mileage challenges. Ultramarathon races are cycling events over long distances and many days, in which the clock keeps ticking. The fastest rider wins, and riders must manage how many stops for food or sleep they take in order to complete the course.

ENDURANCE FOR ALL?

The most famous endurance stage race in the world is the Tour de France, which covers 21 stages in 23 days, over around 2,200 miles (5,540 km). However, this is a race for men only. The UCI Road World Championships have separate races for men and women over the same distances, although bizarrely, the women's course has fewer hilly climbs.

SETTING GOALS

How do riders go from cycling 100 miles (160 km) to cycling several thousand? The answer is that they set goals during training. For example, if their goal is 200 miles (322 km), they add 10 miles (16 km) each week until they reach that goal. To be ready for a specific race, they draw up a plan of weekly total mileage goals using a calendar, working back from the date of the event. That way they can gradually go the distance.

Riders tend to break long-distance races down into chunks in their head, so they focus on tackling one stage at a time.

GIRL TALK

One tactic for winning an endurance race is drafting. This is when a cyclist hunkers down and cycles behind another rider. This saves the back rider energy because the air pushes back on the front rider, not on them. Another is breaking, where a rider sets off on their own to put distance between themself and the rest of the pack.

The main group of riders in a race is called the peloton. Riders are up close to each other but can draft to save energy.

The Long Game

The key to endurance racing is training and preparation. It requires great dedication to be ready to cycle for so many miles for so many hours or days.

BUILD FITNESS

Any cyclist planning to enter an endurance event should spend up to 16 weeks beforehand strengthening their aerobic fitness. The goal here is to be able to handle hard rides better and use up energy reserves more efficiently. The training can be done in different ways for variety and effectiveness. Most should be lower intensity, or slower, over a longer distance, but some should be high-intensity intervals (short bursts of faster cycling) over shorter distances.

Endurance races last many hours, so it is no surprise that training for them takes a lot of time and effort.

Doing planks is a great way to develop some of the core strength that helps endurance racers cope with hours in the saddle.

OUT AND IN

Cycling outside is much more pleasant in better weather and on roads where the traffic is quieter. However, in many places, traffic is always bad and weather during some parts of the year is cold, wet, or windy. That is why endurance cyclists go down to the gym not only to train on stationary bikes, but also to do some weight training to build up arm and core strength.

TIMING TRAINING

Many endurance cyclists plan training times to maximize effectiveness. For example, they may plan very long cycling trips with a steady pace at the weekend or another time when they are not working or studying. Some even ride threshold sessions. These are cycling fast for an hour or more before breakfast to help burn fat in their bodies. However, it is not a good idea to do this without consulting a qualified coach.

GIRL TALK

Hydration is vitally important for all cyclists. They use up water for all body functions, but especially through sweating and breathing out hard. Cyclists should carry a bottle of water attached to the frame of their bike, but they also need to stop to drink more at pit stops during the race. To stay hydrated, many cyclists set a regime of taking a drink every 10 miles (16 km) or 10 minutes, which they measure on their trip computers.

Without enough water, cyclists can get tired, have headaches, and risk getting sick and possibly crashing.

Taking It to the Limit

Endurance cyclists take their bodies to the limit in their sport. Staying on a bike for hours is testing for anyone, so they must be properly prepared for the challenge.

PROPER PREPARATION

It is vital for cyclists to get their bike checked over. This involves lubricating all moving parts, inflating puncture-proof inner tubes in tires, and making sure electrics, such as lights, are working properly. Riders may carry waterproofs for wet weather and high-energy bars and other snacks. Some top racers have support teams to carry spare supplies, too.

ENDURING THE RACE

Experienced or not, it is easy to get saddle sore. Endurance cyclists need to wear cycling shorts made of material that prevents friction between the thighs and with a padded seat to cushion the contact with the saddle. Most female endurance racers have special saddles shaped for women. They are wider at the back as women generally have wider hips than men, and have a cutout to relieve pressure on the sensitive area of the crotch.

GIRL TALK

Mental strength can make the difference between success and giving up in endurance racing. For example, a cyclist may find that a 24-hour race is daunting but much more achievable if they focus on the present and break the distance up into segments. Riders can distract themselves from discomfort in the feet, say, by concentrating instead on wiggling their fingers and thinking about their hands.

Every year, Lael Wilcox cycles around 20,000 miles (32,200 km).

Case Study

LAEL WILCOX—PURSUING HER PASSION

Lael Wilcox is passionate about cycling long distances. She started cycling at 20 years old when she and her boyfriend were traveling around the world. When in Israel, Lael entered her first ultra-endurance race of 1,000 miles (1,600 km) and she was hooked.

Lael Wilcox won the Trans Am race by cycling around 237 miles (381 km) per day for 18 days, and sleeping fewer than 5 hours at night.

A year later, after nine months of cycling on vacation through Eastern Europe, South Africa, and the Middle East, Lael flew back to her hometown of Anchorage, Alaska. In 2015, she entered the Tour Divide. This race spans the length of the Rocky Mountains, from Canada to the Mexican border. Lael may have been considered inexperienced, but she broke the women's record on the Tour by more than two days. She covered the 2,745-mile (4,417 km) race in 17 days, 1 hour, and 51 minutes. In 2016, Lael beat both men and women to win the 4,400-mile (7,080 km) Trans Am Bike Race, a road race across America that allows no support vehicles—cyclists must carry everything they need for the trip.

One of the reasons for Lael's success is that she knows proper preparation is crucial.

Chapter 3

Track Cycling

Track cycling events are big spectator sports as they take place in closed, oval stadiums called velodromes, with banked seating for audiences to watch the spectacle.

IN THE VELODROME

The track inside the velodrome can vary. Tracks have surfaces made from a variety of materials including wood, tarmac, and concrete. Tracks are banked to varying degrees to enable riders to maintain high speeds. Although many people ride velodromes purely for the joy of cycling, there are several events raced there.

The top riders in track races can reach speeds of up to 37 miles per hour (60 km/h).

TAKE YOUR PICK

There are different kinds of track races. For example:

- Sprint: Riders compete over a specified distance and the order of finish determines the winner.

- Pursuit: Teams or individuals start on opposite sides of the oval track and try to overtake their opponents. This does not happen often, so the winner is usually the rider who covers the distance of 4,400 to 5,500 yards (4,000 to 5,000 m) fastest.

- Time trial: Cyclists compete individually against the clock to record the fastest time over the specified distance from a standing start.

- Points race: Points are awarded for specific laps throughout a long race, such as every tenth lap. For example, the first two or four riders will be awarded different points at sprint finishes on every tenth lap.

- Keirin: Between six to nine riders race behind a motorized cycle, known as a derny, gradually accelerating until the last lap and a half, when the derny pulls off the track, and a sprint for the finish determines the winner.

GIRL TALK

Events such as sprints were thought of as sports for larger, muscular male riders because they require short explosive efforts to push to the front at the end of the race. But even in these races, women are competing and winning well because tactics are as important as speed.

In a sprint race, riders need to figure out where to position themselves to have any chance of sprinting to the finish.

Take to the Tracks

All track events demand speed, stamina, technique, tactics, and nerve. Riders also need the right bike and equipment, and they need to know the track they will be cycling like the back of their hands.

TRACK BIKES

Track bikes have a single, fixed gear, meaning that riders cannot freewheel. They also have no brakes, so riders have to slow their pedaling to slow down. Track bikes are built from materials such as carbon fiber, which is very strong, lightweight, stiff, and efficient, and are engineered to help riders achieve ever faster times. Many race bikes have no spokes because these can create turbulence and drag.

GEAR TO GO

Professional riders wear a skinsuit that fits really tightly to make their bodies more aerodynamic, because hundredths of a second can be the difference between winning and losing. For most cycle athletes, two layers of well-fitting sports clothing will suffice, to protect their skin in case of a crash or fall.

Race bikes have no brakes, so athletes are able to ride close together at high speeds without worrying that a competitor will slam on their brakes.

READING BETWEEN THE LINES

Olympic standard velodromes have 820-foot (250 m) wooden tracks with colored bands painted at intervals up the track, which riders must get to know:

- The apron is the flat area between the infield and the track, where riders build speed before progressing onto the boards.
- The light blue painted boards signal the edge of the track.
- The gap between the black line and the red line above it denotes the shortest, and therefore fastest, way to cover the length of the track.
- A darker blue line halfway up the track, also called the stayer's line, is a safe spot to cycle for riders not actively engaged in a sprint. It is often used by pacemakers—riders who set the pace for faster members of their team and then drop back.

The colored lines on the velodrome have a vital role to play in any track cycling race.

GIRL TALK

Track helmets are built for speed. They look a little strange because they are designed to be incredibly aerodynamic. This means that air flows around them easily and quickly to reduce the air resistance that can slow down a cyclist.

Track cycling helmets are shaped to cut down wind resistance and help riders hit their top speed.

Crossing the Line

There was a time when there were more men's track events than women's, but today, in most championships, men and women are on an even footing.

MAIN EVENTS

At the UCI Track Cycling World Championships, there are currently 20 events: 10 for men and 10 for women. Track cycling has featured in every modern Olympic Games except one, and there are currently 10 track events at the Olympics. Women's track cycling was first included in the Olympics in 1988. At the 2000 Olympics in Sydney, Australia, the sport was moved to an indoor track.

Today there are just as many women's track cycling events as there are men's.

GIRL TALK

As well as competing in regular track races, riders also use tracks as a venue to attempt speed records. One of the most famous distance-time records is the Hour Record: what distance a cyclist can cover in one hour, from a standing start. The current holder is US cyclist Evelyn Stevens, who clocked 29.81 miles (47.98 km) in February 2016 in Colorado.

Case Study

JENNIFER VALENTE—STAR OF THE TRACK

Jennifer Valente was born on December 24, 1994, in San Diego, California, where biking is a way of life for many. She started riding around her neighborhood on mountain bikes and a BMX at an early age. In 2008, Jennifer began taking classes at the San Diego Velodrome and started racing about a year later. By 2011, she was not just entering races, but winning them, too!

Jennifer won 12 national and one world junior title during her successful junior career, and then at the 2011 and 2012 Junior Track World Championships, she won three medals, a gold medal and two bronze medals (in the keirin). In the individual pursuit, she won a silver medal at the 2015 UCI Track Cycling World Championships. In the team pursuit, she won two gold medals at the UCI Track Cycling World Championships and a silver medal at the 2016 Olympic Games in Rio de Janeiro.

As well as cycling, Jennifer keeps fit and strong by swimming, body surfing, and paddleboarding.
As well as being physically strong, Jennifer is a race winner because she is also a strategic thinker.

Jennifer Valente was part of the gold-medal winning women's pursuit team at the 2018 UCI Track Cycling World Championships.

Chapter 4 Mountain Biking

While track cyclists enjoy the challenge of repeated racing around a velodrome track, some women prefer to escape into the hills and tackle the trails and rough tracks of mountain slopes on a mountain bike.

Mountain bikes have fat tires and suspension to help them roll over obstacles like rocks and tree roots.

WHAT IS MOUNTAIN BIKING?

Mountain biking is a great way to travel off road and explore wild places. Mountain bikes are rugged bikes with knobbly tires that can ride over mud and gravel, and through shallow streams and rivers. Part of the thrill for mountain bikers is reaching the top of a hill and being able to speed down a challenging descent, sometimes over rocks and around obstacles, such as trees in wooded areas.

WHERE TO MOUNTAIN BIKE

Mountain biking, unlike its name suggests, is not just for the mountains. Cyclists can mountain bike anywhere in the great outdoors. For adventurous cyclists with a map or global positioning system (GPS), they can explore wild places without tracks. Other mountain bike venues have clearly marked and graded trails to follow, starting off with easy routes and gradually getting more difficult with bigger bumps and jumps.

THE BIKE

Mountain bikes have multiple gears. To cope with cycling up high hills, mountain bikers try to use their gears as often as they need them to help keep up their speed. They try to plan ahead–so that if they see a slope coming up, they are ready to change down into an easier gear before they start climbing. Mountain bike brakes are powerful, but as riders rattle down hills, they try to keep their braking gentle and controlled, because they want to keep safe but need to continue going fast to keep their momentum.

GIRL TALK

Bikers tackling high slopes should check the weather forecast before setting out. The weather can change suddenly up a mountain, and storms and winds can be extreme. If there is any suggestion that bad weather is on the way, they should be sensible and postpone their ride.

At the end of a long climb, hardworking mountain bikers are usually rewarded with spectacular views.

Riding High

To be successful at mountain biking, riders must be flexible on their bikes. They have to be ready to move forward, backward, and off to the side at any moment. On a road bike, riders can sit and cycle, but as a mountain bike moves over rugged, ever-changing terrain, riders need to keep changing their position to handle the bike properly and stay on it.

TOP TIPS

For those who are learning the sport, experts suggest that they keep their head up and look at where they want to go. Riders who watch obstacles rather than routes often end up riding into trees rather than avoiding them! On a descent, riders stand up on the pedals and keep their arms and legs bent so they can absorb the shock of the bumps. When riding downhill, riders should also keep their weight toward the back of their bike to avoid tumbling over the handlebars. They keep their fingers over the brake levers so they are ready to brake when necessary. To turn a corner, riders stand up, keep their knees bent, and lean the bike underneath them to turn. This allows them to make the turn but also to keep their weight over the tires so they grip the trail.

Mountain bikers need to learn to ride while keeping a careful watch on where they are going.

WHAT TO WEAR

As well as a good helmet, mountain bikers need gloves. These will help improve their grip because bouncing over rocks and rough ground can make holding onto the handlebars particularly challenging. Being thrown off the saddle and bumping down again suddenly can be made more comfortable by a pair of padded shorts.

Wearing the correct gear keeps riders safe on mountain tracks.

GIRL TALK

Mountain biking gives a rider a whole-body workout. Riders use their arms, shoulders, and core muscles as well as their legs, so the more they ride, the more toned and strong those muscles will become.

The effort of hurtling down tracks on a mountain bike develops riders' strength and muscles.

KIT TO CARRY

Mountain bikers heading out for a long ride should carry a backpack with water, snacks, a cell phone, a waterproof jacket, and a small first aid kit. Mountain bikes are hardy, but even tough bikes can get damaged by the wear and tear of life on rocky trails, so all mountain bikers should carry repair kits. They should know how to fix a punctured inner tube and a broken chain.

Showing Up the Guys

Many mountain bikers like to hit the slopes for fun. Others want to compete in races. Mountain bike racing has categories for all ages and abilities, from short, fun races to long mountain bike marathons and even world contests at Olympic level.

RACE DAY

There are many different types of races. Cross-country races vary in length and are run on multiple laps of a cross-country course. These often have 100 competitors starting at once, so getting a good grid position and a great start is vital. Downhill races take speed and raw nerve. Riders get practice runs to learn the course, then they do timed runs to find the best riders. The top riders then do the run again to find the winning rider. Four cross races pit four riders against each other, racing elbow-to-elbow on a track.

GIRL TALK

Olympic mountain biking, a cross-country race over rough terrain, became an event for men and women at the 1996 Olympic Games in Atlanta, Georgia.

Some mountain bike tracks are specially created for Olympic races to provide a technical ride for the world's best cyclists.

Case Study

KATE COURTNEY—BORN TO RIDE

Although she is just in her early 20s, Kate Courtney is one of the top up-and-coming female cross-country mountain bikers in the world. Kate was destined to be a champion. Born on October 29, 1995, in Palo Alto, California, she grew up riding tandem with her father in Marin County, the birthplace of mountain biking. Kate was competing in mountain bike races by 2009, and won the XC Junior National Championships the very next year. After that, she racked up win after win in national and world events such as the Pan-American Championships and the U23 World Cup (2016).

MENTAL TOUGHNESS

Kate credits her success to gaining mental toughness. At the cross-country race at the UCI Mountain Bike World Championships in 2018, she was in the lead when her tire hit a rock and exploded, causing her to crash at 25 miles per hour (40 km/h) on gravel. Although she was injured, she quickly fixed her tire and got back on the bike. By the end of the race, she had fought her way up to second place.

Kate's dedication and determination helps her to prepare for her aim of winning a medal at the 2020 Olympics in Tokyo, Japan.

Chapter 5
Dirt Jumping

Some mountain bikers leave the trail behind and go dirt jumping instead. This exciting sport is all about the jumps—to get high in the air so that riders can show off their amazing tricks.

The aim of dirt jumping is to get the bike high enough to impress with bold tricks.

MIGHTY MOUNDS

Dirt jumping is a sport where cyclists get air mostly by riding up sloped mounds of dirt. The mounds are set in sequences in dirt jump courses. Riders often land on another mound or an angled slope after jumping the gap in between. The mounds are typically around 6 feet (1.8 m) tall with gaps between them of around 12 feet (3.6 m). The height and gaps vary, depending on the speed riders go up the first mound. If they go faster, the mound can help them jump higher and farther.

GOING HIGHER

Riders need enormous mounds to generate enough speed to make the biggest jumps, with airtime to complete the trickiest tricks. Some places they ride have very steep wooden slopes shaped a bit like those used by ski jumpers. The rider freewheels down and then reaches the first mound at a great pace. The only trouble is they have to push their bike and walk up wooden steps to get to the top of the slope again!

THE TOUGHEST BIKES

The bikes used for jumping need to be super tough to stay intact after high jumps at speed. Their grippy tires have puncture-proof, and sometimes even Kevlar-reinforced, inner tubes. They have small, tough frames, very few gears, and just one brake. More breaks would just add weight and not be used. The bikes have hardtails, or no suspension, at the back, and very firm front suspension. This delivers the right balance between absorbing the shock and riding out of a landing to prepare for the next trick.

GIRL TALK

Flying high in the air at speed increases the risk of sometimes missing a landing and hitting the ground hard. That is why dirt jumpers wear full-face helmets with extended peaks to keep their faces from smashing into the dirt. They wear long sleeves and pants, as well as Kevlar palm gloves to help protect their skin when they fall.

In dirt biking, riders generally jump higher and longer than in mountain biking, and throw in some awesome tricks while in the air.

Dirty Tricks

To dirt jump, riders need guts and determination. Most often they do not achieve or land the next trick without hours of training and preparation.

DIRT DESTINATIONS

The go-to place for learners is a facility such as a skate park. Indoor ones can be used in any weather without the risk of skidding on wet surfaces. At a typical park, there will be not only qualified instructors, but also other dirt jumping enthusiasts with whom riders can share tricks and tips. A standard setup includes various mounds in different sequences, some with narrow edges where riders take off (called lips) and some with wide, flat lips. Small mounds called rollers are useful to ride over to help gain speed before hitting a steeper ramp. A trail path between the jump regions will curve around with banked sides so riders can keep going at speed when changing direction.

It takes great courage to vault high into the air on a bike, but mostly it takes hours and hours of practice to become a great dirt jumper.

WIPEOUT IN SAFETY

Daredevil dirt jumpers take risks because they have practiced all elements of their tricks, including what to do when they wipe out, or fall. This is a normal part of their sport. They learn to jump between mounds over pits that are filled with foam or air bags. If they fall in, they will not suffer serious injury. Over time, the riders also learn to crash in a more controlled way. For example, to avoid any danger of neck injury, they roll out of a forward fall over the handlebars, ensuring their shoulder rather than head contacts the ground.

GIRL TALK

Most mountain bike riders or BMX trail riders like dirt jumping. This is because jumps are a normal part of such trails that riders must negotiate while riding a varied course. While trail riders focus on a smooth, flowing style from jump to jump around a course, dirt jumpers are all about the most mind-boggling tricks they can do. For them, the course is simply a means to set these up.

Dirt bike tracks are designed to allow riders to gain as much momentum as they can so they can jump high and use their airtime to perform crazy tricks.

Airborne Antics

Dirt jumpers pull off some amazing tricks on their mountain bikes while airborne. Along with jump height and length, the most extreme antics are the ones that will score maximum points and win competitions.

TALENTED TRICKSTERS

Here are just a few of the most outlandish tricks that riders pull off in the air before landing safely:

- Superman: Riders take their feet off the pedals and extend them backward so they look like the superhero Superman.
- Cannonball: This is like the Superman, but riders hold onto the saddle with both hands.
- ET: Like the characters in the 1980s movie, riders pedal forward while flying.
- Suicide no-hander: In this trick, riders put their hands behind their back while their legs pinch the seat.
- 360: Riders rotate their bike and themselves one full turn horizontally, until facing the same direction again.

COMPETITION TIME

There are competitions and meets for dirt jumpers worldwide, at a range of different abilities. The world's best professional riders compete at events such as the high-profile Crankworx World Tour series in different countries. There are many other competition series, such as Dirt King in the United Kingdom and the Deutsche Freestyle in Germany, that have both professional and open events for riders of all abilities.

There are legal and unofficial dirt jump areas in many towns that are well away from busy roads, often maintained by the riders themselves.

GIRL TALK

Getting into dirt jumping can immerse riders in a supportive community of like-minded freestyle riders, be they BMX and mountain bikers, or skateboarders.

Case Study

GEMMA CORBERA—NO FEAR OF FLYING

Gemma Corbera from Barcelona, Spain, used to be into rollerskating. But then, one day when she was 17 and skating near a local bike park, she saw some dirt jumping and knew she had to give it a try. That same year, she performed her first backflip and started riding exhibition and downhill races. Gemma had to take two years off of the sport after she was injured in a car crash, but soon got back in the saddle.

Gemma loves the joy of making big, crazy tricks. In 2015, she became a team rider at the Masters of Dirt event and completed a backflip in a 30-foot (9 m) jump.

Gemma Corbera hates to fall during tricks but believes that taking risks and sometimes failing are key to learning her sport faster.

Gemma performs at many events not just in Spain, but around the world.

Chapter 6
BMX Girls

One of the biggest stories in the BMX biking world in recent years has been the rise of female riders. These BMX girls are taking the racing and freestyle scenes by storm and riding better and faster than ever before.

BMX RACES

BMX is short for bicycle motocross (motocross is off-road motorbike racing), and BMX races take place on purpose-built off-road, single-lap racetracks. In most cases, a BMX track has a starting gate with places for up to eight racers, a winding dirt race course that contains various jumps and bumps, and a finish line. The starting gate is on a raised bank, and the riders lean their tires against the gate as they wait to drop in.

When the gate opens, riders launch themselves down the starting hill, which helps them pick up speed. They jostle for the best positions and go from 0 to 40 miles per hour (0 to 64 km/hour) in seconds. The rest of the track is usually flat, about 15 feet (4.6 m) wide, and with large, banked corners that help the riders maintain speed.

BMX girls are taking the biking world by storm!

BMX racing is one of the fastest, most exciting sports for cyclists to compete in.

BMX TERMS

A BMX track is made up of hills and bumps riders must work through while maintaining a high speed. These hills and bumps have specific names:

- Berm: This is a 180- or 90-degree turn on a bank. Taking the right path on a berm can help a rider get ahead of their competitors.

- Double: This is two hills spaced just far enough apart that the fastest route is to jump through the air between them.

- Step-up: A step-up is a short hill, followed immediately by a larger one. A step-down is the opposite of this.

- Roller: A roller is a single small hill or a group of small hills.

- Rhythm section: This is a combination of hills and jumps.

Challenging, purpose-built tracks like this really put BMX riders through their paces.

GIRL TALK

BMX racers have to balance speed and aggression with safety. For example, hustling too roughly to take the lead on a berm can lead to contact and a nasty spill.

In It to Win It

BMX races are big news and, since 2008, they have even been part of the Olympic Games. An average BMX race lasts for about 30 to 40 seconds, depending on how fast the riders are and what the course is like. There is a lot of excitement packed into that short time!

RACE DAY

A BMX race is typically divided into three parts: time trials, qualifiers, and the final. In a time trial, each rider races the course alone against the clock, to decide what seeding they will take in the first competitive stage. The qualification heat stage consists of quarter-finals and semi-finals, with the top four riders at the end of each round progressing to the next round of competition until eight riders have eventually qualified for the final. The final is the main race, in which the riders fight for glory—and medals.

Female BMX riders had a chance to show off their awesome skills at the Rio Olympics in 2016.

GIRL TALK

The BMX Olympic final features the top four riders from each of the semi-finals, and only consists of one race. The winner is the person whose front wheel crosses the finish line first.

Case Study

ALISE WILLOUGHBY—THE BEAST

Despite being short in stature, Alise Willoughby's competitive nature and incredibly fearsome racing skills have earned her the nickname of "The Beast." In 2006, she became the first woman ever voted Rookie Pro of the Year by *BMXer* magazine, as well as the youngest to win the American Bicycle Association (ABA) national title, at age 15.

Born on January 17, 1991 in St. Cloud, Minnesota, Alise started racing at the age of six because her brother raced and suggested that she try it too. She panicked at her first race after looking down the steep starting hill, but the following week she overcame her nerves and came second. When she was just 15, she turned professional and gained her first win at the ABA Supernationals in Desoto, Texas, that same year.

Alise has had her share of physical challenges, enduring several surgeries, but she bounces back every time. She has taken part in two Olympic Games, placing twelfth at the 2012 Olympics and bringing home a silver medal at the 2016 Olympic Games in Rio.

Alise got her "Beast" nickname as a joke because of her petite size, but the name fits because she's a rebellious rider who is a real daredevil.

BMX Freestyle

Freestyle is where BMX riders take to the air and do awesome stunts and tricks on their bikes. Whenever BMX women hit the bike park, you can guarantee they are going to put on a show!

BMX freestylers are not interested in riding from point A to point B, they want to get creative doing old tricks and finding new ones.

STYLING IT!

Freestyle BMX is an extreme sport that consists of five disciplines:

• Street: Street riders make use of urban and public spaces to perform tricks. These tricks can be performed on curbs, handrails, stairs, ledges, banks, and other obstacles.

• Park: Park riders use skate parks to put their bikes through their paces.

• Vert: Vert is performed in a curved valley, which consists of two quarter pipes set facing each other (much like a mini ramp), but at around 10 to 15 feet (3 to 4.5 m) tall.

• Trails: These are paths with jumps made of heavily compacted, or pressed, dirt.

• Flatland: Flatland riders use only smooth, flat surfaces, such as parking lots and basketball courts. They perform tricks by spinning and balancing their body and bikes.

AIR TRICKS

Flatland riders specialize in tricks they can do on the ground. Their bikes have four pegs, one either side of each wheel, so riders can stand on them to do tricks. In the steamroller trick, a rider stands on one side of the bike on the front pegs, leans forward over the bars to kick the back end round, until the bike is at 180 degrees, and then grabs the seat. In most other styles of freestyle BMX, riders aim to get air—to jump their bike and do tricks, spins, and flips while they are in midair.

BMX freestylers love to take to the air!

TAKE IT SLOW

People often learn to BMX freestyle by watching friends or downloading video tutorials. The key to success is building up the skills slowly. They usually start with something basic like a bunny hop, in which they ride slowly, lift up the front tire by pulling up on the handlebars, and then push the handlebars forward while in the air to lift up the back tire, too.

Some people say flatland BMXers look like they are breakdancing on their bikes.

GIRL TALK

With freestyle making its debut at the 2020 Olympics in Tokyo, BMX girls are finally hitting the main stage and progressing their skills in major world tournaments.

Tricks and Turns

Talented BMX riders become legends in the sporting world for their daring and dangerous tricks. They do a huge number of different stunts, some of them similar to those done by dirt jumpers and other stunt-bike athletes.

TRICKY NAMES

Some of these acrobatic feats have crazy and memorable names, and there are BMX tricks starting with almost every letter of the alphabet. For example, these are some of the tricks starting with the letter T:

- Tire grab: The rider grabs their front tire.
- Toboggan: The rider releases one hand from the handlebars and grabs their seat, usually turning the handlebars to about 90 degrees.
- Tuck no hander: The rider tucks in the handlebars and takes off both hands.
- Turn down: The rider whips the bike out to one side and turns the handlebars into their legs, wrapping them around their leg.

There is a massive range of tricks BMX freestylers can choose from to impress the crowds who watch them.

Case Study

HANNAH ROBERTS—TEEN SENSATION

Hannah Roberts first climbed on a BMX bike when she was eight years old to try to follow in her famous cousin Brett Banasiewicz's tracks. Since then, her high-flying tricks have made her one of the best BMX freestyle riders in the world.

Hannah's training involves about 40 hours a week at the skate park. During the school year, she rides after class and all day on Saturdays and Sundays. When she travels to competitions, she takes all her books, teachers email her notes, and she tries to get homework done while on the road.

Hannah's advice to other female riders is: "Don't ever give up before you try—you never know what's going to happen until you give it a shot."

TRAIN HARD TO WIN

The training seems to be paying off. Hannah has won everything that could possibly be won in women's BMX. She won the Vans BMX Pro Cup, the UCI BMX Supercross World Cup, and the UCI BMX World Championship, and has her sights set on the 2020 Olympics.

Although men still outnumber women in BMX, Roberts has seen a rise in the number of girls getting into riding and hopes to see even more.

GIRL TALK

All BMX bikes are lightweight and durable to make them easier to lift into the air and capable of surviving the impact of landings. Depending on the type of freestyle BMX, the bikes are made of different materials and have slightly varied shapes.

Becoming a Supergirl

Have you always wanted to set out on the open road, speed around a velodrome, scramble down a mountain on two wheels, or get muddy on the dirt trails? Whatever cycle sport interests you, do not be put off by the idea that these awesome activities are just for boys. More and more girls and women are jumping into the saddle and taking on a new challenge. Have you got what it takes to become a sporting supergirl?

TAKING TO TWO WHEELS

Sporting supergirls are not just those people who make it to the top of their game and win medals and prizes at competitions. Learning to do any extreme cycling sport will make you fit and strong, and give you the belief that you can succeed in anything you dedicate your time to. These are the things that matter and that make a true supergirl.

GIVE IT YOUR ALL

Some sporting supergirls do cycle sports for fun; others participate to compete. Those who want to enter and win competitions need to put in a lot of time and effort. Winning takes dedication and determination and may mean you have to give up a lot of your free time to become really skilled. However, the rewards of seeing your techniques improve make any hardships worthwhile.

Some supergirls win medals, but others get different benefits from their sport.

CYCLE TOWARD A NEW CAREER

Some people turn the sport they love into a job. Those who are good with people might want to become coaches or mentors, passing on their knowledge and enthusiasm for biking. Other cycle sports careers include designing bikes and cycling gear; organizing events, championships, and games; promoting competitions to tell the public about them; and writing reports and reviews about athletes or events.

GIRL TALK

To learn more about your chosen cycling sport, you could speak to a few different people who do the sport or people who train cyclists. You could also watch videos of the sport you want to try. Even if a style of cycling looks challenging, it is worth giving it a try!

Trying a new sport is your chance to learn a new skill, get in shape, make friends, and have fun.

Try It Out!

Find out just how great girls can be at all kinds of sports—then find your inner supergirl and try them out for yourself! There is a wide range of exciting cycle sports to try, so there is sure to be one that suits you.

Regardless of what you are into, whether it is long-distance or endurance biking, cycling track races, mountain biking, dirt jumping, or BMX, there are plenty of clubs around the United States that you can join to learn about cycle sports.

ENDURANCE RACING

Find out if there is a cycling club near where you live by visiting the USA Cycling website at:
https://legacy.usacycling.org/clubs

TRACK CYCLING

If you would like to try racing at a velodrome, go to:
https://legacy.usacycling.org/velodromes-in-the-us.htm

Visit the Centers of Excellence website to find club programs that encourage young rider development at:
www.usacycling.org/foundation/centers-of-excellence

MOUNTAIN BIKING

Locate the best US ride centers, with extensive trails for all abilities, designated by the International Mountain Bicycling Association at:
www.imba.com/ride/where-to-ride/ride-centers?param=ride-center

To find out if your state has a local association that organizes mountain biking, check out:
https://legacy.usacycling.org/la

DIRT JUMPING

You can find like-minded dirt jumpers at the centers listed on the Extreme Sports Map at:
www.extremesportsmap.com/mtb

BMX

If you would like to go to summer camp to learn street BMX, try:
www.campwoodward.com/summer-camps/action-sports/bmx

Check out the locations of BMX tracks for training and racing at:
www.usabmx.com/site/bmx_tracks?section_id=13

Cycle sports are a great test of your endurance and stamina.

GIRL TALK

Once you know what sort of bike sport you are into, research some clubs. Speak to a few instructors to see whose class you would like to join, then find out what you need to do to improve, such as gym work or hours on the road. Get expert advice on the best bike to buy on your budget and what safety equipment you will need. Then try some classes or training sessions. Often you can try before you pay. Remember, even if a sport looks challenging, it is worth giving it a chance—you are there to learn a new skill, get in shape, and have fun!

Glossary

aerobic exercise that makes people breathe hard and the blood pump faster through their veins as it carries oxygen to the muscles

aerodynamic smoothly shaped in order to move through the air more quickly

air resistance the force air exerts against a moving object, slowing it down

banked sloping

circuit a roughly circular track or route

core the muscles within the torso

cumulative increasing by one addition after another

disciplines different fields or types of a sport

drag the force air exerts against a moving object, slowing it down

durable long-lasting

endurance the ability to keep doing something for a long time

freestyle a competition or sports style in which there are few rules about moves and techniques

friction the force between two objects that are sliding, or trying to slide, across each other

global positioning system (GPS) a navigation system that uses signals from satellites and math to determine an exact location

handicaps disadvantages given to someone who is a better rider, in order to make the riders in an event more equal

hydration the process of absorbing water

impact the force of one object hitting another

infield the area inside the track

inner tubes air-filled tubes inside a tire

Kevlar a strong, man-made fiber

lubricating using oil or grease to prevent parts of a machine sticking or rubbing

mentors people who give someone younger or less experienced help and advice

momentum the force that keeps an object moving after it has started

professional doing a particular activity as a job rather than just for fun

publicity advertisements, posters, and other things that attract the attention of the public

seeding a ranking given so that the best riders do not meet until the end of a tournament

staggered arranged so that things happen at different times

stamina physical or mental strength that allows people to continue doing something for a long time

suspension the system of springs and shock absorbers by which a vehicle is supported on its wheels

tandem a bicycle with pedals and seats for two

terrain an area of land and its features

turbulence unsteady movement of air or water

For More Information

BOOKS

Daynes, Katie. *Cycling* (Usborne Spectator Guides). New York, NY: Usborne Publishing, 2016.

Katirgis, Jane, and Ellen C. Labrecque. *Racing BMX Bikes* (Speed Racers). Berkeley Heights, NJ: Enslow Publishing, 2018.

Whiting, Jim. *BMX* (Odysseys in Extreme Sports). Mankato, MN: Creative Paperbacks, 2018.

Whiting, Jim. *Mountain Biking* (Odysseys in Extreme Sports). Mankato, MN: Creative Paperbacks, 2018.

WEBSITES

Discover more about mountain biking at:
https://adventure.howstuffworks.com/outdoor-activities/biking/mountain-biking.htm

Find out more about cycling at the Olympic Games at:
www.olympic.org/cycling-road

For some amazing tricks that came with years of practice, watch this video:
www.redbull.com/gb-en/projects/frames-of-mind

Learn BMX tricks at:
www.wikihow.com/do-BMX-tricks

Publisher's note to educators and parents:

Our editors have carefully reviewed these websites to ensure that they are suitable for students. Many websites change frequently, however, and we cannot guarantee that a site's future contents will continue to meet our high standards of quality and educational value. Be advised that students should be closely supervised whenever they access the Internet.

Index